A DOG'S GUIDE TO LIFE

LESSONS FROM "MOOSE"

By Jack Cotton

Illustrated by Deb Hoeffner

With love for Ann Marie, Melissa,
Andrew, and Maxwell.

Copyright 2006 Jack Cotton
Published by Tide-mark Press, Ltd.
P.O. Box 20, Windsor, Connecticut 06095-0020

Illustrations by Deb Hoeffner
Text design by Paul Rasid

ISBN 978-159490234-5

Second Edition/Second Printing

Printed in Korea

Preface

Our black Chevy Tahoe sped down the highway, testing the upper boundaries of the speed limit. The mood inside the car was somber. Moose, our Boykin Spaniel, was stretched out on a blanket in the way-back of the car. His eyes were glassy, his coat dull, and his breathing was slow and labored. In the back seat, my son and his friend kept a watchful eye on our very sick dog, whispering words of encouragement.

Just an hour before, our vet had called to say that after four days in the local hospital, Moose now needed to be taken to a better-equipped facility, and as quickly as possible.

As we whizzed past highway markers, I reflected on what this little dog had meant to our family. We've all heard the saying that a dog is man's best friend. In this case, Moose was a dad's best friend.

As a single father trying to make joint custody work, I brought Moose into our lives as a puppy some nine years earlier. He had made the difficult process of shifting the children between homes a lot easier. Over the years, he was an integral player in many happy times. He especially loved the outdoor shower and samples from the grill. The main focus of his attention was the burgeoning squirrel population in our yard. Several times each day, a carefully calculated attack ended in a breathless standoff between Moose and a squirrel, locked in odious stares from ground to treetop.

I thought about the blessings of the wonderful relationship I had with my fabulous kids, and I realized how much I owed to our little friend who was now suffering in the back of the car.

After he passed, I wanted to write something about Moose for my children, Melissa and Andrew, to remember him by. I also wanted our newborn son, Maxwell, to get to know him. The lessons contained in this book center on Moose's little quirks—some typical of dogs, some not. They flowed from a sense of his loss and my intense love for my children. I think of these lessons daily and try to live by them. I sincerely hope you will enjoy reading them.

—Jack Cotton
Cape Cod, Massachusetts

Lesson 1: Begin every day with excitement and anticipation.

They say that dogs have no sense of time. I can't be sure. Even though the day-to-day routine didn't change much for Moose, he was always up at the crack of dawn, ready for action or for something new to enter his world. Any day could have been the one when a squirrel would be caught, a long-forgotten bone would be found, or a ride in the car would await him.

Lesson 2: Love unconditionally.

I'm not always in the best mood.

I sometimes get stressed, irritated, or just plain cranky.

Hard to believe, I know.

This never affected Moose. He was there with a smile,

a nuzzle, or a lick every time, without fail.

I'm not sure humans can accomplish this,

but it's a great goal!

Lesson 3: Smile.

I can't swear that Moose was really wearing a smile all the time.

He may have been just panting with his mouth open.

It's a dog thing, I guess.

It looked like a smile to me, though, and perception is reality.

No matter what kind of day I had, he met me with that smiling,

panting face. Imagine the change we could make

in the lives of others if we always wore a smile.

Lesson 4: Be enthusiastic.

For the nine years of his life, Moose barked and ran to the door

if someone came to visit. Not once was the visitor for him.

Nevertheless, he treated each knock of the door or ring of the bell

as though it were the first and was never disappointed when it

turned out the visitor had come to see someone else in the house.

He was gracious in greeting them, and then he returned

to his previous occupation.

Lesson 5: Arrive early.

Moose always looked forward to my time in the outside shower.

He could get his face washed and maybe catch a tennis ball

in the summer or a snowball in the winter.

Although I usually got there by about 7:00 A.M.,

he was always ready and waiting by 6:00 A.M.

I'm not saying you should always be an hour early for everything—

just a little bit early.

Otherwise, you never know what you might miss.

Lesson 6: Never, never, never give up.

We've all noticed the drastic increase in the squirrel population.

It is very noticeable in our yard. Moose would wait, watch, hide,

and stalk—not for hours, but for years.

At the moment he judged best, in a burst of speed

and with bits of torn grass or deck splinters flying,

he would charge toward his prey.

In nine years, we never saw him actually catch one,

but he never stopped trying.

I know he would have succeeded if he had had more time.

How often do we give up after one or two tries at something?

Lesson 7: Take a nap in a sunny spot.

Work, appointments, and schedules can cause stress,

and stress is a part of our daily lives.

Every now and then, imagine how it would be to find a nice,

warm spot, maybe by a window, a fireplace,

or on the lawn, and just snooze.

There is no better way to reset the stress meter

we all carry within us.

Lesson 8: Get up to greet those you meet.

Moose was never one for a casual greeting.

Even if one of us returned from a five-minute absence,

he always got up and extended himself for a warm greeting.

As humans, we can get lazy and complacent in greeting one another.

Make it a habit to give a warm welcome

to those you care about. Imagine the effect.

Lesson 9: Live in the moment.

Again, this is probably a dog thing. Moose never seemed stressed and

certainly seemed able to find joy in every thing in every moment.

We, on the other hand, are always stressed.

Ninety percent of our stress comes from worrying about

what happened in the past or what might happen in the future.

There is nothing we can do about either one.

While worrying, we often miss out on what's happening right now.

Focus on the joy of the present.

Lesson 10: Drive with your windows open every now and then.

I don't know what it is with dogs and open car windows.

Maybe long ears feel good flapping in the breeze.

Mine are a little bit big, but they don't flap.

All I do know is that in these days of air conditioning,

hermetically sealed rooms, and thermopane windows,

we need to feel the rush of air in our faces from time to time.

Don't risk an accident with unsafe driving, but next time you're

sitting in the passenger seat of a car, open your window,

and feel the wind in your face, even if just for a few minutes.

Lesson 11: Leave some food in your dish.

Moose was fed at about the same time every day.

He never finished off the bowl during his first go at it.

Even though his feeding routine didn't change much

during his nine years, he always saved a bit in the off chance

I might forget to refill it the next morning.

Whether it's food or the fruits of our labors,

it's always good to save a bit, just in case.

Lesson 12: Take time to sniff.

Moose had his own door and kept his own hours.

Occasionally, though, leash in hand,

we did the dog-and-master thing.

My goal on these excursions was mostly aerobic.

His was to drink in each of the wonders of the world as we traveled.

Okay, his goal was to sniff everything, tugging annoyingly

on his leash as he stopped.

Of course, we should not forget our goals and destinations.

At the same time, it's good every now and then

to stop and "smell the roses." Maybe not every two feet,

but more than just once in a while.

Lesson 13: Make a difference.

Moose was around during some tough times in our family.

His presence relieved tension, eased transitions, and soothed hurt feelings.

While he might have been a pain from time to time,

our family and the little world in which we live

are immeasurably better for his having been a part of them.

It may not have been his goal, but it should be for each of us:

to make the world a little better for our having been here.

Lesson 14: Remember that you never know when it's the last goodbye.

Dogs have no concept of a master's return. They think every time they see you leave, you are not coming back. Dogs get very sad over this, and if it were up to them, there'd be only long goodbyes. Even in what turned out to be Moose's final days, I never really thought I was saying goodbye for the last time each time my hospital visit ended.

Since I was not able to be with him in his final moments, I wish all the more that I had lingered a bit longer on what turned out to be the last goodbye. Whenever you say goodbye to someone you love, make it count. With God's will, it won't be the last one. One time it will be, though, and you don't want to be looking back, wishing it had been more.

About the Author

Jack Cotton works full time in the real estate business he founded in his
Babson College dormitory room more than thirty years ago.
Jack, a native of Cape Cod, can't imagine living anywhere else.
He and his family reside in a small Cape village
with a yard now overrun by squirrels.

About the Illustrator

Deb Hoeffner specializes in people and animals
in the traditional mediums of watercolor, pastel, graphite, and oil.
Her work has appeared in magazines, books, prints, stamps, products,
and various collectibles over the course of her twenty-year career.
Deb has a master's degree in fine arts with continued studies
at the Art Students League, Parsons, the School of Visual Arts
and many European art museums. She has recently relocated
to a beautiful new studio in Buck's County, Pennsylvania,
which she shares with her rather exuberant collie, Emma.